MY NEIGHBOUR PEEJAY

To marilyn
+ Jeffery
Lots of love

Lynskylee

2004

MY NEIGHBOUR PEEJAY

Lyndsylee Spence

iUniverse, Inc.
New York Lincoln Shanghai

My Neighbour Peejay

iUniverse, Inc.

For information address:
iUniverse, Inc.
2021 Pine Lake Road, Suite 100
Lincoln, NE 68512
www.iuniverse.com

ISBN: 0-595-30962-3

Printed in the United States of America

Isn't it strange how one measly thing can alter your life and make you grow more precautious of frail looking pensioners? You are probably wondering what I am blabbering on about. I shall let you in on a secret; no body knows this secret but me, Betty Poodle. My neighbour Peejay is a thief! Well I haven't actually witnessed her stealing anything but I have watched her attempt robbery. No, she was not trying to steal the crown jewels like any professional, or greedy thief for that matter would, she is trying to steal my dad. Yes, I know what you are thinking, would an adult no be aware of some one was trying to steal them? The fact is, no my dad has no idea, in fact to look at Peejay, she looks frail and lonely, but behind her peering green eyes is a cunning brain, a brain all too dangerous for anyone to analyse. Peejay is like a spider, she observes her prey then lures it into her web that is why I have to stop her!

Strangely enough, summer is the most dangerous time of the year. Not because the pollen levels are high, or wasps are on the loose or even your dad wears his embarrassing knee length shorts, but for the simple reason, Peejay has an excuse to lounge in her garden without any hesitation what I or the other neighbours think. As the sun peeks up through the trees, like laser beams burning her eyes, Peejay is up at the crack of dawn while most wise people are still snoozing and dreaming of hot chocolate sundaes with sprinkles and whipped cream. Naturally, being the most cautious member of my family I rise early too, only not as early as my double crossing, deceitful neighbour. I must be alert at all times just in case Peejay has any ideas.

Whilst I am standing in the kitchen being as silent as a mouse I will hear a gradual creek and a slam that is how I know Peejay is outside. Without looking too much like a spy I pretend to butter my toast as I watch Peejay arrange her deck chair in a perfect angle for a magnificent view of my dad, some day I will grow a business brain and charge her an hourly fee, after all she is treating my dad like a side act. Too bad vaudeville or floorshows are not back in fashion. They are in my remaining family members little world. Now I remember what I had to tell you. You see I come from a weird family. Of course being a caring person I adore them but this is really strange and you must solemnly swear not to laugh when I tell you about them. My mother is called Clara Kitten and my father is called Jeffery Jewels (Jeff for short). Now, I know what you will say 'so what! You're name is silly too!' Yes, I am aware that Betty Poodle is no modern name and I sound like a circus act. But you are missing the moral of the story. My parents are stuck in a time warp! Yes, that's correct the year is 1955 well in my house anyway! The only flaw is, I am not stuck in their little world of moon burgers, 'I love Lucy' and Elvis Presley! Too bad we would make a great team. In case you did not know, the fifties were a time of youth and innocence. My parents are going through what I would call a mid life crisis at the moment and are mourning their youth so the only logical thing to do is revisit it.

Peejay looks at this downfall as a chance to snatch my dad as she knows he is at his most vulnerable.

My mother thinks Peejay is divine 'such a sweet lady' she will remark. Sweet! She is far from sweet; she is in fact one bad apple! Mother is, well shall we say 'a push over' poor mother caught up in an era, confused and innocent, just as well a levelled headed, modern person like I is around to catch her when she falls down. Dad is in the same situation as mother, they need to wake up and smell the Chanel no. 5 and realise they are living next door to an ex convict!

Your eyes are not deceiving you, I did say convict. Peejay spent a great deal of time in prison, in fact so long that she forgets how to behave in a civilised manner. This experience has left her bitter and she wants dad to be as wired up as she is. That will not happen as long as I am around to keep tabs on what she is up to. Okay, so you think, the lady has done her time behind bars she has learnt her lesson and will not break societies laws again! However, I think that her prison days taught her a few lessons. The wrong kind of lessons in my opinion, the only thing she has learned is every trick in the book!

Getting back to summer, I have already told you about the door creaking and the positioning of the deck chair but what I failed to mention was her summer wardrobe. Okay, so the dame is old, that means high neck woolly sweaters, sensible shoes and a good coating of factor forty to prevent sun burn. Peejay is the complete opposite. Try an outrageous straw hat perched on top of tangled grey hair, a bold Hawaiian shirt held together with safety pins, beige safari shorts that hang down to her knobbly knees, striped knee socks and ridiculous brown Moses sandals. Peejay will make an entrance by strolling over to her deck chair, and draping her hunched over bag of bones figure onto the chair, she will then place huge opaque sunglasses over her eyes 'to prevent the sun from damaging her cataracts' more like so dad is not aware that she is staring at him as he mows our manicured lawn. Her idea of heaven is relaxing in her garden and smoking a menthol cigarette with the aid of a black cigarette stick just to add a little glamour to her haggard appearance. Every now and again an ice cold beer will appear in Peejay's hand. Fresh from the cool box she will grad it and bites the metal cap off with her canine fangs as she sips the alcohol she sighs in content as dad parades around the garden. Please do not get the wrong impression. I do not loath Peejay in fact she is quite amusing when she tells her made up stories. My parents believe them but I do not.

I think my favourite story that Peejay told me is about her wild jazz parties back in the jazz age of flappers and prohibition. She would begin with 'once upon a jar of moonshine' and it would cascade into how she was the most beautiful flapper with the sleekest bob and grooviest Charleston moves on the dance floor when one fateful night whilst partying hard at the kit Kat Club back in old Manhattan Al Capone wandered in like a lost soul and noticed Peejay who at the time had an alias of Zelda Stardust dancing in the footlights in beat with the music. Mr. Capone then walked over and offered her a glass of bath tub gin and as we say the rest is history. Every night he would take her to his old pal Rudolf Valentino's pent house on Park Avenue and they would mingle with Mary Pickford and Theda Bara who Peejay claims was the 'spitting image' of in her younger days as a New York socialite. She would then progress into a web of lies about how Hollywood begged her to make a screen test but she refused because she did not want to steal the spotlight from any hopeful young starlet. This is one of the rare occasions that Peejay makes her old age evident.

On the other hand I know she is lying. How could anyone so undignified become a New York socialite, I mean who would invite her in for triangle sandwiches with tea in china cup? She would scoff the sandwiches, slurp the tea and probably drop the expensive delicate cup! I feel that the whole experience would be a culture shock!

Speaking about food and basic table manners I really must tell you about the time we were eating outside and Peejay made an entrance. Dad was slaving over a barbecue while mother was in the kitchen making a salad. 'What ya cookin' Jeff?' Peejay wrapped her spider like fingers over the fence and barked. I observed this from the patio where I had a wonderful view of the whole situation. Dad being his neighbourly self promptly lifted a sausage with his new utensils and kindly gave Peejay it. 'Oh Jeff!' she gasped 'I would kill for a man like you!'

'Hmm' I thought 'Kill eh?' That got the wheels into my head clicking; you could almost smell the burning of my brain cells in action. Perhaps Peejay is going to kill mother or else hide her in the attic so she can have the privilege of dad cooking for her every night. This got me frightened, I knew I had to warn mother but I had to approach her with caution. Casually walking into the kitchen I leaned against the wall and said in a rather calm voice 'mother do you think Peejay is odd?'

'Odd?' she asked confused 'why do you ask dear?'

'Well, she is a little unbalanced but besides that I fear that she will kill you some day to steal dad' I blurted out without warning, so much for giving a firm but reassuring speech about my neighbour

'Betty Poodle! I am shocked' mother said as she pickled the beetroot 'what possessed you to say such a thing about darling old Peejay'

'I heard her say something like 'I would just kill to have a man like you Jeff' I said overly dramatic

'Oh, it's a figure of speech; Peejay is just lonely and misses her husband'

'Where is Peejay's other half?' I asked not really wanting to know

'She said the mafia killed him' mother answered

'The mob killed Mr. Peejay?' I asked in astonishment 'oh my sainted aunt that's even worse than her Al Capone tales' I left the kitchen because I was getting no sense at all out of mother, maybe I should back off a little and try to take everything in my stride, even her eccentric vocabulary. I knew I needed to take more action and investigate more into the whole ordeal but that could wait all I wanted to do was eat my dinner outside in the blazing sun without developing a freckled nose from the sunlight.

Waiting impatiently for my dinner I pondered over practical matters in my head. Perhaps when every one is fast asleep I could sneak out of bed and spy on Peejay. Wait! Is that not what we law abiding folk call trespassing? And isn't looking through someone else's window invasion of privacy? Maybe so, but my dad is at stake and no measures are to extreme to protect my family when the sun has gone down I shall take action!

Finally dinner was served all that was lacking was tomato ketchup. Well into my dinner, in a little daze as I devoured my hotdog I heard a high pitch sound come from Peejay's direction. It is the type of tune one cannot describe in words. But hey, I shall give it a go. I had heard the music before, oh yes, now I remember the summer I vacationed in Cuba I often danced to the tune, it was in fact the Rhumba theme tune, very exotic and fun, until at the side of my eye I saw a vision of bright colours swaying. I turned my head in the colourful direction and saw Peejay dressed up in a tall zany hat sporting a wide range of fruit attached to it. Her dress was purple with pink ruffles and grapes pinned in all corners of it and her shoes were pointy pink boots with buttons going along the sides. Above the blare of the music she roared as she moved her arms back in forth in a distracting motion; you too could have a body like mine if you Rhumba' and with the end of her sentence she started to shake from head to toe. Quite disturbing and her dancing put me off my dinner. Thanks a lot Peejay; because of your little quirks my appetite has to suffer. From past experience I thought all old people were meant to be sweet and give you cookies not shake their booty in front of you and give you the evil eye. But what is ordinary about my life anyway? Isn't eccentricity the essence of living or maybe peaceful neighbours is but who knows because I certainly did not write the book about life?

That evening as I was helping with the washing up I asked mother a question 'Mother why did Peejay disrupt our dinner this evening?'

She seriously answered 'attention problems.' That truthful answer got me thinking. You know maybe mother was not such a prehistoric fool and perhaps in her mercenary little mind she is aware of Peejay's little schemes but is in denial. How sad I guess it is up to me to help solve her problem and get rid of Peejay for good. You know maybe alligators do have the right idea after all, they eat their young.

That very evening when the world was sleeping I crept out of bed and changed out my nightclothes into an outfit of black. Equipped with only a torch and my fading courage I snuck out of the house and into Peejay's garden. A flickering light was beaming from behind her curtained window. The first thing that popped into my mind was 'blow torch' Peejay is going to come and burn us alive! Quick hide Betty Poodle! But oh no I had my brave head on that day nothing was going to hold me back no barriers thick enough could stop me. Look out Peejay I am coming to spy on you. Getting back to the curtained window, at first when I seen it closed I felt like a failure because I could not see inside, but this is where my 20/20 eye sight is an advantage. A minuet little slit was left open where the two curtains joined, a gap wide enough to peep inside without your silhouette being caught by the light from inside. Carefully I leaned down to be at eye level with my new spying tool. Easy does it, do not fall against the window and distract dozy old Peejay!

Once in a spying position I began to study Peejay's inside surroundings. Nothing uncommon about her living room, it consists of a settee, two chairs and a television. Oh wait the television caught my attention; it was playing a black and white movie. I could tell the movie was an old war time tear jerker because of its musical score usually starring Cary Grant who always wins the girl at the end. Maybe old Peejay doesn't plot to win dad all the time, maybe today she is being sentimental but the film was good. Also having very good hearing I could listen to the dialogue, it was very simple. The actress I noticed was the Swedish star Ingrid Bergman, oh wait a moment it was the video Peejay borrowed off mother and dad titled 'Casablanca' ah ha! It is all fitting into place now! Peejay has had the video for months now I am sure by now she has seen it already. Oh hold on a second here comes that famous scene where Humphrey Bogart says 'Here's watching ya' Oh no do I see tears? Is that tough old Peejay crying? Golly marbles it is! She does have a heart, deep down inside that hallow bony rib cage there is a human beating heart with a soft spot for old films.

Now I am totally distracted but intrigued. Okay Betty Poodle, Peejay is infatuated with the film it is safe for you to get more confident and look closer into the window. Uh oh I did not see that happening, geez why could Peejay not rake the leaves up in her garden I just slipped on them and smacked my nose off her window now she is going to really resent me. Oh I am an old fool literally.

Quick! I tried to lower my head but my static hair was still in total view. What's that thumping noise, like an earthquake? I peeked up and there was Peejay approaching the window. With no apparent fear of who might be lurking outside she threw open her curtains and peered out. The light from inside shone down on me and I ran like an Olympic athlete. Through her thorn hedges and over her barb wire fence but I made it, with great stamina and boundless energy I was finally home.

Totally out of breath I burst threw my door. Oh dear, not the discrete entrance that I had planned previously that evening. Nothing I could do now, the front door had slammed and suddenly I felt a presence behind me. Still dressed in my black outfit and stocking cap I turned around and there was dad froze in a pose with his left arm raised equipped with a bat. 'Ahhhhhhhh' I shrieked 'dad it's me!' I warned in case I inherited a black eye!

'Betty Poodle! What on earth are you doing' he quizzed. 'I was out for a walk' I answered quickly. I knew I had to act fast but cool at the same time. It is best not to raise suspicion. 'At three in the morning?' he scanned his watch in the dark. 'Oh yeah dad, you know me, always walking!' I shrugged the question off with foolish optimism.

Careful not to wake mother I removed my shoes and silently crept to my room. That night I made an important discovery, not very ordinary considering my family life. The fact is that I actually enjoyed the adrenalin rush of spying on Peejay with the high risk of being caught! Oddly, after my slight mishap of nearly being caught in my mind I knew it was wrong but my childish conscience was encouraging me to repeat it another time. You know what? I think I will!

Morning had finally come although I did not rise until noon. That is understandable because I did not make it to bed until after three in the morning. My fault of course. Perhaps I need a hobby! Walking down my creaky stairs I heard my name being called. I wonder who it could be. Oh yes, I recognised the voice it was mother. Will she punish me or did she even know? The answer, she did not have the slightest recollection of what happened, maybe dad did tell her but she thought it was best to have a guilty conscience as punishment instead of being fed bread and water for forty days! I had totally forgot about spying on Peejay again until I heard her unmistakable voice coming from outside. Is the old bat talking to herself? Wait a moment, no she is not, I hear mothers voice to! Maybe Peejay is telling her about the intruder. Quick look innocent!

'Clara Kitten!' Peejay hissed 'do you wear perfume?' Peejay pronounced Perfume as *Puuuurrrrrfffffoooooooommmmmmeee.*

'Yes, occasionally' mother answered as she sipped her tea 'why do you ask?'

'Oh shucks can't a person ask a civilised question these days?' Peejay growled 'One last thing does Jeff buy you perfume?' If you listen carefully you will hear that Peejay says Jeff *very* softly.

Ending that sentence my dad drove up to our house and Peejay scurried!! How odd, Peejay usually greets dad with a huge smile displaying her rotten yellow fangs and an exaggerated 'Good after noon Jeffery.'

Betty Poodle beware! Old Peej' is up to another cunning plan!

It was about noon, dad was unwinding in the garden after a long days work at the office. Reading his paper and minding his own business a foul aroma tickled his senses. Dad lowered his newspaper below his nose and started to sniff. Suddenly he followed the stench and noticed Peejay standing, well should I say, leaning against the fence all dressed up! Yep, that is right. She was not in her ratty torn old clothes but in a cocktail dress, well an attempt at a cocktail dress visibly hand made, a lot of pancake make up, in fact so much she looked like a dead clown!

'Hello Jeff' there it was, the different voice I was telling you about

'Good afternoon Peejay' dad was not paying any attention of this silly old woman and continued to read his newspaper.

Impatiently Peejay barked 'Jeff' and dad flinched 'yyyyeeesss' he stuttered, I could almost hear his scared heart beating off his ribs.

'Do you like my perfume?' she whirled and twirled to make the unbearable scent travel.

'The smell!' dad thought aloud with his eyes glazed over 'that's the smell! Clara Kitten I told you not to use weed killer in the garden, you know how it effects my sinuses!'

Ending on that note, Peejay petulantly stormed off into her den of a house. That harsh reaction to her homemade perfume did not discourage her. Without warning she sprung a surprise on us the very next day.

'Good morning Peejay' mother cheerfully called over to Peejay who was sun bathing in her garden

'Oh shut up' I heard Peejay mutter 'Hello dear!' she called aloud in a depressed voice

Hmm the old girl is looking for a sympathy vote to help her forget the perfume act.

'Anything wrong?' mother asked

'Oh darn I forgot to tell you' she tossed her hand in our direction 'it's my birthday today didn't you know?'

'Really!' I answered pretending to be pleased 'you know Peejay you should have told us sooner; maybe we could have arranged a party'

'Betty Poodle is always trying to make situations' mother laughed my spiteful comment off

In a child like voice Peejay mimicked mother 'Betty Poodle is always trying to make situations' and in a harsh voice she mumbled 'the little toe rag.' Naturally mother did not hear any of this.

Mother went back inside; I stayed in the garden and pretended to be busy whilst the whole time I observed Peejay. Okay, so I am not Sherlock Holmes but I can put two and two together and get something out of it. My imagination was synthesising each time I glanced in Peejay's direction. Casually she sipped a bottle of beer through a straw as she munched on crackers. Nothing too odd for a snack but is it not a little early in the day for alcohol, even for Peejay? She must really be depressed. Oh how awful! Poor old Peejay depressed that means no more wacky behaviour and most of all no more stories. Now I feel sad because she feels sad and when I feel sad mother feels sad and when mother feels sad dad feels sad! Oh no a vicious circle of sadness make it stop!!!

Wait, hold on a moment! What was that I just witnessed? Could it be…yes…it was! Oh it really was a little smile. Not a friendly smile but an evil smirk, you know one of those devious side grins that tell a thousand words. Listening careful as I peeked through the cracks in the fence I could hear the wheels in Peejay's imagination going *Click…Click…*a little slow at first but then it speeded up and I heard *click, click, click* and to top it all off steam started flying out of her ears and her hair stood on end. Ah ha! I knew it was too good to be true she is not sad she is plotting something. Something that I do not know what the outcome will be, but I do know something, I must keep guard and be ready!

Anyway, later that day, well afternoon to be precise mother and I were planting some flowers when Peejay snuck up behind us and said 'Hey!' a sound straight from her diaphragm. 'What in heavens name…' I began to say just as I realised who the predator was. 'Oh hello Peejay' I patronized a sickening smile 'how are you feeling now' I managed to say between my toothy grin.

'Never mind how the hell I am' she hissed back 'I just came to tell you that I am having a birthday bash tonight at seven o'clock and Jeff, you and that brat, excuse me, I mean darling little girl are cordially invited but be sure to buy me a chic gift or else…' and with that she strolled away singing to herself. Is she forward or not? Who in the right mind invites people to a party and then demands a gift? Not just any gifts mind you, but a chic gift! What is Peejay expecting, Tiffany silverware? Some people have a nerve!

Talking about nerves, does your mother ever rattle your cage sometimes? I thought so, mine too. Mommy dearest decided to go shopping for Peejay's gift. Yes, that does sound like a thoughtful gesture but the catch is, I had to go too. Why could she not just put some gift vouchers in a birthday card and wish her well? Some people never learn.

Getting back to the subject of shopping, I did not go with my own free will no that was vanished when she lured me into a common trick that is used on silly children like me.

I was in my room doing nothing in particular, yep just what I thought, the bored are vulnerable. 'Betty Poodle' I heard someone call my name. 'Yeah?' I called back.

'Want to come to the shop with me?' it was mother calling me 'sure! But how come?' I asked back

'You can get candies' I heard the word 'CANDIES' oh woohoo I love sugar! I practically fell down the stairs trying to put my shoes on as I ran down them two at a time. The young are so enthusiastic! It's quite misleading in way.

I knew I was not seeing things when we drove straight past the candy store. 'Hey!' I yelled 'the candy store!' I pointed at the distant store. Mother ignored me and kept driving 'earth to mother' I mocked 'where are we going?'

'Oh darling sorry I guess we'll just have to keep on driving and visit the candy store after' she replied

'Where the hell are we going?' I got the point

'To buy a present for Peejay and watch your language please'. Language!! You have not heard language, just wait until I get cranky then I will have so much language it will make your hair stand on end!

Golly marbles what a great start to the day, having to go shopping for some insane neighbour who resents you! All I can say is that mother is very forgiving. If it was me who was purchasing the gift I would tar and feather Peejay as a gift.

Inside the store I became restless. What do you expect? It was a grown up clothes store. You know the type? I bet you do, full of high neck sweaters, sensible shoes, decent length skirts and cardigans that make you itch. My plan to escape came to a halt when I heard a voice screeching like a cat. "Moon river wider than a mile' was the lyrics I heard and when I turned around the weirdest thing happened. No, Peejay did not jump out of a rack of clothes, but mother was singing. Really dreadful singing that drew attention to her.

'Mother will you kindly be quiet' I said pretending to be the wisest person out of us two.

'Oh Betty Poodle I just adore this song I could sing all day!' mother swayed her head from side to side as she continued to sing.

'Okay you keep singing if it makes you happy but we need to get you home for your medication' I said aloud so everyone would think mother was crazy.

The onlookers thought this was very funny and disguised that they were watching by rummaging through racks of clothes. Although, I knew they were watching that is the reason why I spoke louder than usual. The scene was over and mother had wandered off to the pensioner section. I crept up behind her and mimicked Peejay. 'Hey!' I grabbed her shoulder and startled her.

'Found anything yet?' I asked uninterested.

'Oh wait a moment…yes what do you think?' mother held up a pink cardigan with little buttons on it.

'It would be nice for a sweet aunt but Peejay would be better off with a bottle of beer' I commented

'Oh Betty Poodle' she said as though she was lecturing me all day without success 'Peejay is not at all bad, I don't know why you look for the bad in people'

'Well' I gave a sly look 'Peejay is fond of the old jazz and liquor.'

So, after trying to convince mother into leaving the cardigan and buy Peejay a bottle of beer I was very exhausted. Mother did, however, buy the cardigan and I never got my candy. Tough luck Betty Poodle nothing ever turns out the way we hope it will.

The highlight of my afternoon was spying on Peejay, shopping for Peejay's present and my mother singing. Aren't I a lucky girl?

Now, for the highlight of my evening, to tell you the truth I do not really want to recall the events leading up to Peejay's party or her actual party. Nightmares will haunt me forever and I have been scared for life!

'Come on you two!' mother scolded us for being very much disorganised; I do not think dad wanted to attend either as he is not a sociable person.

'I'm ready' I answered back

'Hurray for that now let's get going' Mother grew more impatient as I stalled.

'As the singing ship sailed into the sinking sand we say good night to free will and happy thoughts' I chanted hauntingly with over exaggerated gestures.

Mother armed with an attractive pink wrapped gift wearing a huge ribbon was obviously Peejay's birthday surprise, I walked slowly behind dad. Finally after a two minute walk to Peejay's house, which seemed like a two hour walk might I add, we had finally reached her driveway. Ah! The driveway now that's a death-trap if there ever was one, each step I took, I tripped over loose gravel and pot holes. She really was out to get me and there was nothing I, or anyone else could do about it. The music was turned up very loud because we could hear it from outside. After minutes of rapping Peejay's front door we heard *thump, thump, thump*, no it was not the music.

'What'd ya want?' Peejay growled from inside.

'Hello' mother called nervously through the letter box 'it's Clara, Jeff and Betty.' The front door swung open and there was a vision of white. No it was not the angel of peace, it was Peejay in a white jump suit with gold buttons, large shades with gold rims and white loafer shoes. She struck a pose, very disco glam rock era, with one hand pointed in the air and the other one down she was an image that would discourage anyone from watching John Travolta's films.

I wanted to laugh out loud, I really did. Oh, you should have seen her or should I say it. Peejay was a sight for sore eyes. Still holding that ridiculous pose she said 'well you're here you might as well come in.' Mother anxiously gave her our present and with such a greedy force Peejay snatched the beautifully wrapped gift out of mothers arms and tore the pink wrapping paper open. Mother watched close to tears as Peejay ripped the paper to shreds and tossed the ribbon into the bin. It had been mother's favourite hair ribbon and now it was gone. 'A stupid cardigan?' she ungratefully peered up. Mother, dad and I watched traumatized by her reaction. 'You could at least say thank you' I told Peejay.

'Shut up!' she snapped 'I'm the birthday girl and what ever I say goes! So where is the card?' she asked.

'On the floor underneath the shredded wrapping paper' I answered sarcastically. Maybe my snide comment and shrewd tone of voice would be enough to make Peejay feel guilty for upsetting a terribly sensitive lady like mother. You could not have been more wrong Betty Poodle!

Peejay's eyes scanned the card conscientiously and breaking the awkward silence she glanced at mother threatening' why isn't Jeff's name on it?' she demanded an explanation.

'Jeff chose the card' mother answered trying not to offend Peejay or upset her.

'Oh' she stared at dad with a gleam in her eyes and a huge smile stretching from ear to ear she gasped in a sweet voice 'then I shall value it even the more.' Dad gulped in fear. Maybe he wasn't so naïve about the whole situation after all; did he know all along what Peejay was up to? Did he know she was insane? Or did he not want to upset her again? Compliment on his side or a threat on my side? I cannot figure it out.

Time had rolled on, and no one knew what to talk about, mainly because Peejay was in a fragile mental state and anything negative might set her off again. Actually we had only been there ten minutes and we left. Mother was on the verge of hysterics, dad did not know what to say and I was afraid of lashing out at Peejay. Personally I know Peejay was drinking, and I don't mean orange juice she also smelled of smoke. Perhaps it was best to leave and let her think about the spectacle she had once again made of herself.

'Good bye Peejay and thank you for having us' mother never could hold a grudge.

'Have a nice birthday' dad managed to say

'Drop dead' I hissed and gave a huge smile when mother look in my direction.

Peejay rose to the occasion once again and stood on her door step waving a cigarette 'Farewell fellow neighbours.' Then her door slammed. Bet you can't guess what Peejay did that night?

Yes, that is right she probably got drunk with her secret stash of liquor, excuse me, I mean bath tub gin.

As soon as we three returned back to our house mother and dad breathed a sigh of relief whilst I went daft. Shouting criticisms about Peejay and this time mother did not make any effort to defend her either. Dad just sat silent and read. It was late so we all went to bed and the funniest thing happened. I remember falling straight asleep and then all of a sudden, without any warning I sat up and heard scraping noises. First I did not think anything was wrong, but drunk with fatigue and in a trance I walked over to the window. Oh gosh! What is that out there? I shone my torch into the garden. There was a small black figure digging a hole in the garden next door. That is when I realised the black figure was Peejay on her hands and knees in the full moonlight and *she* was digging the hole! Maybe she is planting a few flowers...no wait a minute the hole looks about six feet deep. Uh oh! Hide Betty Poodle she is aware of the light. Well of course she is because I was shining it down on her. How foolish, just like the window scene that happened previously I had to hide and hope for the best. But why am I hiding? I mean, I am in my own room behind double glazing windows and my front door has about a million bolts on it. Anyway if I am so afraid, and I admit it, then it shows the psychological damage Peejay is doing to my mind! And if that is not a reasonable explanation then it proves that curiosity is getting the better of me!

Now, this is the strangest part of the evening. Peejay started to howl at the moon. Quick! I should just let her howl and hide under my blankets. No, being my nosey self I had to investigate.

Peejay saw me! Maybe she will ignore me; I should be so lucky she dropped her shovel and waved her fist in my direction. Torture! One of these days I am going to freak out and blow her cover!

That night, I could not sleep at all! I pondered over solutions and conclusions in my mind. My only explanation for Peejay's erratic behaviour was that she was going to find a way to get rid of mother and me so she can live in harmony with dad! Over my dead body, tomorrow I shall tell the others.

I woke early in the morning, well I dozed off but my brain told me 'get up Betty Poodle, go down stairs and warn your parents' and that is precisely what I did.

'Mother and dad I need to tell you something but please don't get mad' I calmly told them

'Oh no' mother held her hands to her face and I said excitedly 'you already know?' phew, at least I did not have to go into a song and dance about their lives being at stake. 'You did not smash Uncle Fred's urn did you?'

'Uncle Fred, who the heck is he?' oh yeah I quickly remembered my mothers uncle who lives in a vase thing in the living room. 'Oh no mother I didn't Good old Uncle Fred is okay, the fact is you and dad aren't' I spat the words out quickly.

'Honey have you been eating too much sugar again? Dad asked

'No, no not at all' I threw my hands up in the air, 'it's Peejay she is going to kill us!'

'Betty, no one is going to kill us, now just you sit down and relax and I'll phone the nice doctor to come over and examine you' mother tried to assure me.

'No, it's true, quick look outside!' I shouted in defence

'Oh, look Jeff Peejay got one of those water features that you wanted last summer.' Oh darn, now mother and dad have gone insane too. I peeked out the window, and right enough, she had a garden feature, in fact it was right where she was digging last night. Was I seeing things, did I imagine Peejay digging? Now I doubt myself, that is the first sign of denial and I cannot let Peejay win. I get her idea, a back up plan, the water feature is to disguise the hole, well like fun it will. Just as soon as I get dressed I am going into that garden to move *that* feature and we'll soon see who is lying.

Jeepers, is that Peejay knocking at my door? I think it is.

'I'll get it!' I called. It was something I had to do, face my demons or demon for that matter. I opened the door, my hand was shaking but I managed to say hello.

'Hi Peejay what do you want' I abruptly asked not sparing her any time to patronise me or harass me.

'Oh talk about a reoccurring nightmare' she glanced at me 'where's your mother?' Peejay pushed past me and stormed down the hallway to the living room.

I faintly heard mother say 'Good morning Peejay what can we do for you? What a lovely skirt is that new?

Mother can make me feel sick sometimes, she is too nice and compliments everything. Seriously, I could walk up to her wearing a crumpled up old potato sack with nut shells as earrings and she would say 'my, darling what an attractive outfit.' Maybe I should make my self scarce today, I am being too negative and I know I'll lash out at Peejay. On the other hand, I am going to sit outside the door and listen in. Using the oldest eavesdropping trick, I pressed a glass up against the wall and put my left ear again it. The coldness tickled but this was no time to burst into a fit of laughter. The only part of the conversation I caught was 'Hell, Jeff and Clara I am extremely sorry for my ironic behaviour last night, I was so depressed about my age I took it out on you!'

'How old are you Peejay?' dad questioned, Oh dad, what a daring question, you never ask a lady that! But, then again Peejay is not a lady. I will give you a quick pardon for that.

'Thirty one' Peejay answered quickly. I almost fainted. Thirty one my eye! More like one hundred and thirty. How could some one with a million wrinkles and grey hair be thirty one? That is just the height of nonsense, not unless Peejay did not age well.

'Oh, I am just joshing' Peejay roared with laughter 'had y'all fooled didn't I? I know I look younger than what I really am but you didn't have to believe me!' I could just imagine dad's shocked expression; I bet his eyes are like saucers and his eyes brows are up around his hair line.

The more revealing topic was mentioned and thoroughly discussed. Yes that is correct, the genuine sickening conversations, relationships. 'Where is your husband Peejay?' mother dared to ask. This answer better be good, because my ear is getting frost bite from being pressed up against a cold glass. 'Dead' was Peejay's brief answer 'a fatal accident in the garden'

Mother sympathetically replied 'how awful, you must really miss him'

'Oh gawd don't get my started, we'll be here all day!' Peejay puffed on one cigarette after another. After a short awkward silence Peejay began her story. 'To make a long story short, Ricardo, that's my husband, he always disrupted my gardening to fetch him thing if it wasn't a shot of brandy it was to get his medication, well I set my spade down after digging a deep whole and went to fetch his pills, I have had peace of mind since.'

'Was it the hole? Did fall down!?' dad inquired. Dad, don't look too interested because it will encourage Peejay to hang around even longer.

'Yes' Peejay sighed 'it was the hole, completely his fault, if he had worn his glasses he would not have tripped over the spade and into the hole, it serves him right, I always told him that once day Karma would come along and bite him in the ass.'

So that's where he is, I always thought the scarecrow in Peejay's backyard resembled her deceased husband! Now I know where he is, he is a scarecrow in her garden, talk about keeping it in the family!

'I can read your mind' she stared at dad 'yes the scarecrow is a replica of him, I didn't like him so I pasted a picture of his face onto the scarecrow, now the birds can peck his brains out,'

Mother fainted with the smell of Peejay's cigarettes. All the smoke whirling around the room took advantage of mother's vulnerable sinuses and went straight to her head.

'I regret to inform you that I must leave' Peejay announced as though we had begged her to stay 'I really must go home and read my mail, you know I get hate mail!' She seemed proud of that. 'Okay Peejay we'll be having our dinner soon anyway' dad said eager to get her out the front door.

'What are you having' Peejay asked.

'Steak and kidney pie'

'Mmmm internal organs' and off Peejay went down the driveway.

'Betty Poodle' dad saw me sitting against the wall with a glass in my hand 'what on earth are you doing?'

'Nothing' I answered too quickly to cover my tracks 'is mother okay?' I walked over to mother just as she opened her eyes. 'What…Where am I, what happened? She stared hazily around the kitchen.

'Don't you remember?' I stirred up a great story 'you got terribly drunk last night and you fell asleep on the floor…remember you have a few drinks too many at Peejay's party?'

'I did!' mother was shocked and ashamed 'oh how awful did I make a fool out of myself?'

'Yeah, you were dancing on the table' I pretended to be appalled by her behaviour

'No, you didn't' dad stepped in just on time to ruin my story 'you fainted a few minutes ago because Peejay's passive smoking'

'I did?' mother asked confused

'Yes, she was sitting right beside you smoking, I must admit I felt pretty woozy myself' dad informed her. Finally, Peejay has showed her true colours, a botched up murder story (in my opinion) and making mother faint, once I am finished reminding mother and dad about her erratic behaviour the puzzle will fall into place. Just leave it to me! Even if I have to exaggerate and lie I will convince them.

An event that happened the very next day served as a purpose to change my parents, well at least my dad's opinion on Peejay. You see Peejay just became too carried away with her schemes. For once Peejay's smartness beat my common sense. She had gone to the trouble of waiting patiently for mother to go shopping and then she hopped over our fence. What she forgot to investigate was where I would be. Of course being totally disobedient I was in my room reading silently. I heard our front door creak open, I thought it was mother. Then I heard it close again and footsteps echoing towards the kitchen. How strange, mother must be home early! I could hear clinging and all sorts of rattles going on downstairs. Mother must be making tea I thought. I heard dad come in and I continued back to my reading.

'Hello!' he cheerfully called.

'Just a moment' was a reply, sounding not at all like mother unless she had laryngitis. Suddenly dad's screaming startled me. I ran quietly downstairs and hid behind the door.

There stood Peejay, dressed up as mother. A bad attempt, she was wearing a blonde curled wig over her straggly grey hair, a pink cardigan and a skirt with a million petticoats under it, she must have stolen them off our washing line! 'Peejay!' dad shouted 'what are you doing?'

'What do you mean Jeff darling' Peejay asked pretending to be offended.

'Dad looked around our kitchen afraid. I would have been afraid too because when Peejay gets mad it can be very frightening!

'We belong together' Peejay smiled 'we are a modern day Spencer Tracy and Katharine Hepburn.'

'Peejay I am a married man with a child! Peejay you cannot do this, now leave! Dad protested.

'Go where dear?'

'Home, I want you to go home!' dad tried to push Peejay out

'Just click your heels three times and say there's no place like home' Peejay laughed in dad's face 'I am home.'

Dad saw an angle. A perfect little angle I must say myself, he decided to patronise Peejay and play along with her game.

'Peejay dear' dad played 'please make me a cup of tea'

'Right away' she saluted dad. I was real proud that dad was witty enough to do that. Peejay was making enough noise in the kitchen, rattling spoons and the noise of the kettle was enough to prevent me from eavesdropping.

Peejay appeared with a cup of tea 'Drink up' she grinned.

Dad being good natured drank it in case Peejay turned into a psychopath and took offence. I could see Dad swaying from side to side. His eyes were rolling back into his head. Oh no, he has fell into a deep sleep.

Dad was still sitting in the chair sleeping when Peejay pulled some rope from her pocket. She tied dad to the chair and held him hostage. I began to panic, what if she ties me up too! Then I will be her hostage as well. I crept back upstairs and rang the police and an ambulance 'don't make any sirens' I warned them 'she is very unpredictable.'

I knew we would be safe so I ran into the kitchen and pretended to be shocked.

'Peejay!' I screamed 'what have you done?'

'What ever happened to calling me mother?'

'You are not my mother, my mother isn't ugly and old' I offended her on purpose. Peejay tried to wrestle me to the ground but I kicked her. Peejay's false teeth flew across the room and landed without breaking.

'Made of metal' she boasted 'they call me jaws!'

I could hear automobiles outside and a knock on the door.

'HELP!' I screamed until my throat became hoarse. Of course this was all an act, I wasn't afraid, I was playing a game, just like Peejay, I wanted to look like the innocent child being attacked by an insane old woman.

Two doctors came running in with several policemen; I pretended to be weak from defending myself. 'Help' I weakly cried 'somebody help me'

The doctors were untying dad and putting him onto a stretcher. They just left him lying on the floor to concentrate on Peejay and me. The police men were helping me. They kept questioning me but all I said was 'she tried to kill me' in a low, scared voice 'she tried to kill me'

They asked me if I was okay and I should come down to the station to make a statement.

'No, its fine thank you' I answered and then Peejay freaked out and yelled 'I'll get you!'

'Okay' a policeman nodded to a doctor 'phone them'

'Peejay, she is nuts, she trapped dad' I told them out of breath.

She has been after him for months, she made her husband into a scarecrow too' I informed them just to let them be aware of what kind of lunatic they were dealing with.

'Oh one of those' the doctor nodded

'She is dressed up as mother' I said

Peejay was yelling for attention 'Yoo-hoo, look at me'

'Quick, hide!' I called 'she is going to kill me.'

With perfect timing mother appeared. 'Hello' she called as she walked inside 'what's going on in here?'

'Mother!' I called 'come quick'

The policemen informed mother what had went on and she sat there stunned. Her eyes bugged right out of her head and stared into space as though Peejay had betrayed her.

'Peejay, you are unwell' Mother told her 'if you go away to hospital you will be better soon'

'Shut up you silly fool!' Peejay shouted. Oh dear, Peejay has just offended mother. Now mother is mad and I hope she never forgives Peejay. 'I am going to go in now, but I hope what ever you are searching for, you find it and would you be so kind to return my cardigan and skirt back to the clothes line.'

I was laughing out loud and Peejay pouted. Mother was furious. Now, at last mother and dad believed me. As always, the kid is always right. Never underestimate the power of the child mind.

'Will Peejay go to the nut house?' I asked

'Oh Betty Poodle you really are quite ruthless aren't you?' mother laughed

'Yes, Peejay will be certified' the doctor told us

Mother would go crazy if she knew that I provoked Peejay into attacking me. Honesty is the best policy is her catch phrase. I heard the doctor on the phone.

'Yes, hello, this is Doctor Appletree I have a woman who needs medical attention' a short pause 'yes she does have attention problems, uh huh, right well her name is Peejay Pistachio, yes, she lives at twenty four parachute park.

'The white van will be over right away to pick Peejay up' he hung up. Oh how wonderful finally we are getting peace from Peejay!

Sure enough, about half an hour later we heard an automobile pull up outside and heavy doors slamming. Mother and I ran to the kitchen window. 'There here!' I gasped. We both went outside to watch. The circus had finally come to town when the two men in white coats hauled Peejay out of her door.

'Hey wait a minute!' she yelled 'let me loose!' Peejay put up a fight and it was a struggle getting her strapped into a straight jacket. A nurse walked over and injected her. In perfect timing Peejay's eyes rolled about and she slurred her speech 'dude, I haven't felt like this since the 60s'

'This one needs special attention' I heard a doctor say. Off Peejay went in a straight jacket into the back of the white van. Mother pulled up in the car just as the white van rolled down the street. Surprisingly mother did not make any comment except for a wicked smile. Dad was still lying in the kitchen strapped to a stretcher. He'll be out cold for days I am guessing.

I felt sad as I watched the van drive off in the distance, some how it seemed like the end of an era. And in a way it was. I miss Peejay, I don't know where she is but somewhere, somehow she is preying on her next victim.

Acknowledgments

It was common knowledge amongst my friends that I would write a book, or at least attempt to. Personally I did not think 'My Neighbour Peejay' would be the finished result. I would like to take this opportunity to thank many of my good friends for inspiring me with havoc created scenes that I could use to my advantage to develop a storyline on.

My havoc companion is my best friend Ashley Crowhurst. Ashley always goes along with my ideas, not that she doesn't have a mind of her own because she does, and a very brilliant one too, without being my partner in crime I could not have settled down for a day or two to write this. It was all the havoc that exhausted me into creating this story. Thanks Ashley for being my best friend and encouraging me to 'go for it'.

Matthew Stevenson is my other best friend, I chat to him every-day and each day I talk about my newest projects. Usually his instant reaction is a loud laugh or a rolling of the eyes. That makes me more determined to prove him wrong. Thanks for rolling your eyes Matt.

Amie Baird is the chief creator of the name 'Peejay' without her brain cell getting into full gear Peejay could have had the unluckiness with being stuck with a normal name.

I have been terribly lucky with my sources to find good situations to base this story on. I also have good friends who didn't create any scenes or names but they are not getting away with out some acknowledgement. For instance there is Richard, who should be in show business. All he does is laugh and say catch phrases for example 'let's talk about balloons' to name one of millions. Another Matthew who I also consider a very good friend, he chats all day about things mainly insulting people he dislikes or exaggerating a simple story. Without his insults and exaggeration we wouldn't have our laughs at lunch time. Then there is Ashley's older sister Claire who is one of the best artists and creative people I know. She is a walking piece of art with her unique style and flamboyance that makes the most decorative people look plain. Claire said this story was 'very entertaining' so I decided to publish it. Without Claire's encouraging comment poor Peejay would be in the recycle bin. I would like to thank my great great aunt Clara, in total happiness of her being my aunt I named the character Clara Kitten after my very own Aunt Clara.

Lorraine and Victor my grandparents are probably the biggest influences in my life. My nanny Lorraine could be the original stage mother. She encourages me to go after all my ideas even if they are impossible for example when I wanted to be a Ziegfeld Girl. They dogs Mister Rollie and Millie were like my uncle and aunt even though they were dachshunds. I loved Millie too even if she was temperamental. Humans should use Rollie as a classic example how to behave. Mister Rollie loved everyone and I adored him like my life depended on it. I could pull him apart and he wouldn't show his teeth. Everyone misses Rollie and Millie but now Nanny and Granda have their Yorkshire Terriers Minnie and Fizz.

I am thankful to my parents and Mark for encouraging me to keep writing Peejay because if they didn't, Peejay would only be a character of my imagination.

I would like to extend my gratitude to my other family members around the world including aunt, uncles, grandparents and cousins especially the wonderful people Tanya and Lauren. There are so many people that I want to thank but there isn't enough paper in the world to fit their names onto. Thank you to family friends most especially my New York traveling companion Emma and my neighbour Siobhan.

J'Taime (to everyone)

0-595-30962-3

Printed in the United Kingdom
by Lightning Source UK Ltd.
100460UKS00002BA/4